A BATTLE OF WORDS

Heather Christie

Illustrated by Jacqui Young

Written by Heather Christie
Illustrated by Jacqui Young
Designed by Marina Messiha

Published by Mimosa Publications Pty Ltd
PO Box 779, Hawthorn 3122, Australia
© 1995 Mimosa Publications Pty Ltd

Literacy 2000 is a Trademark registered in the
United States Patent and Trademark Office.

Distributed in the United States of America by

Rigby
A Division of Reed Elsevier Inc.
500 Coventry Lane
Crystal Lake, IL 60014
800-822-8661

Distributed in Canada by
    PRENTICE HALL GINN
    1870 Birchmount Road
    Scarborough
    Ontario M1P 2J7

03 02 01 00
10 9 8 7 6 5

Printed in Hong Kong through Bookbuilders

ISBN 0 7327 1566 0

A BATTLE OF WORDS

A BATTLE OF WORDS

It all began with my birthday present – a great pair of in-line skates. I just couldn't wait to race out and try them – but then, before I knew it, I was accused of – oh, never mind. You read the letters and decide who was right and who was wrong in this battle of words.

16 Crescent Way
September 15

To the Young Female Person residing
at 18 Crescent Way,

This afternoon, at approximately 4:10
p.m.(I was much too shaken to note
the exact time), you EXPLODED from
your gate. In your mad rush,
a hard object struck me, causing me
to drop my groceries. My carton of
milk burst. This resulted in my:
(a) Having to hose down the sidewalk
(b) Having to wash all the groceries
(c) NOT having any milk.

So what do we have?
(a) A waste of water
(b) A waste of time
(c) A waste of milk.

But that's not all. I was looking
forward to a well-earned cup of
coffee. I have never drunk, nor will
I ever drink, my coffee without milk!

Yours faithfully,

C. V. Molesworth

C. V. Molesworth
(Resident and taxpayer)

"Better let me check that letter to C. V. Molesworth," Dad suggested, when he saw me writing a reply. Dad is a court reporter; he knows about "incriminating statements" and things like that.

"P. S. can return some milk," Mom said. "I'll buy a carton to replace the one she spilled."

"*If* P. S. did spill the milk in the first place," Dad said. "We don't know that she did. We only have C. V. Molesworth's word on that."

"For goodness' sake," Mom said. "What's a little milk? All this will blow over once C. V. Molesworth has had a nice cup of coffee."

18 Crescent Way
September 15

Dear C. V. Molesworth,

The carton of milk that comes with this letter does not mean that I admit I am guilty. Mom just thought you'd like a cup of coffee.

I'm sorry you've had so much trouble. The "hard object" you mention might have been my elbow. If it was, I'm very sorry, even though there is NO EVIDENCE that this *was* the "hard object."

Dad says that if I hit you with my elbow I would have felt it. Mom says that I don't feel, see, or hear *anything* when I'm excited. I was trying out my new birthday present, you see.

Yours faithfully,

P. S. McGinnity

P. S. McGinnity (Resident and non-taxpayer)

We haven't lived at 18 Crescent Way very long. It was a "deceased estate." That means the person living here before us died. Mom says he was an old gentleman and it all became too much for him. When Dad tries to cut down the undergrowth, he mutters that it's too much for him, as well, but Mom only laughs and says he needs the exercise. I wish he'd leave it like it is, full of secret places and mossy stones.

C. V. Molesworth's house looks a lot like our place. Even the windows are like ours – which means that they're not exactly sparkling clean.

I still felt a bit guilty about the accident I *might* have caused, and looking at the next-door windows gave me a kind, neighborly idea. I could wash them for C. V. Molesworth!

16 Crescent Way
September 16

Dear P. S. McGinnity,

I can only assume that you find it amusing to hose a person through that person's bedroom window while the person is attempting to take a nap – on doctor's orders. I had not thought from the tone of your previous letter that you would be a spiteful person. I am shocked and saddened.

Apart from being soaked to the skin myself, there is also the matter of a wet quilt and mattress.

I wish Mr. Thomas still lived next door. He would never, under any circumstances, have treated me in such a way. In fact, we never exchanged one single word on any subject whatsoever.

Yours faithfully,

C. V. Molesworth

C. V. Molesworth

"I thought that the window was closed," I said again. "I was only trying to be neighborly and helpful."

Dad looked gloomy. "Now we'll be sued," he said.

"I could put the mattress outside to dry, hang out the quilt, and offer to do odd jobs," I suggested.

Mom nearly exploded. "We have enough odd jobs around *here* to take us into the next century!" (She'd just discovered that the whole house needed new wiring, and she was a bit tense.)

Dad thought for a moment. "P. S. can write an apology, and she can offer to pay the cleaning costs."

"I don't have enough money!" I yelled in alarm.

"Pen and paper, P. S.," Dad said sternly.

18 Crescent Way
September 17

Dear C. V. Molesworth,

A misunderstanding on my part has occurred in the matter of your bedroom window. I thought it was shut. My intention was to clean it for you, not to soak you to the skin.

That's the truth. I am not spiteful, as you think. Mom and Dad will pay for any cleaning, but I hope it's not too much because they're worried about how much it's costing to fix up our place.

I don't want to move. I really love it here. I expect you did, too — before I moved in next door. I'm really sorry for my mistake.

Your unhappy neighbor,

P.S. McGinnity

P. S. McGinnity

"What have you been up to?" Mom asked. "You're a sight!"

I'd wriggled and pushed through a tangle of bushes growing along the fence, but it had been worth it. I'd found some lovely pink flowers.

"I think they might be dog-roses," Mom explained, which I thought was a strange name for them. "Let's find a vase."

"Half for you," I told her, "and half for C. V. Molesworth."

Mom looked uneasy. "I don't know, P. S. – maybe we should let sleeping dogs lie."

Dog roses? Sleeping dogs? With all this sudden talk about dogs, I actually forgot about C. V. Molesworth for a second and wondered if Mom was hinting at something. So far I'd never been allowed to have a dog, but maybe Mom had changed her mind, now that we had a big yard.

I looked hopeful, but Mom only said, "It's peaceful now. I'd like to keep it that way."

16 Crescent Way
September 21

Dear P. S. McGinnity,

I was somewhat surprised to find that a "gift" of my own roses had appeared on my doorstep. I don't like people who give with one hand and take with the other. Stealing, I call it.

You are right. I did like it here before you moved next door. Clearly, things will never be the same again. Now I wake up each morning wondering what new disaster you are saving up for me.

Your worried neighbor,

C. V. Molesworth

C. V. Molesworth

C. V. Molesworth's latest letter upset me a lot. She'd practically called me a thief! I went off and started to cry. I really hadn't known that those pink flowers had been growing through the fence from her place. As if I would have given them to her if I'd realized!

I decided to write one more letter and then follow Mr. Thomas's example and never speak to C. V. Molesworth again. Who would want to?

18 Crescent Way
September 22

Dear C. V. Molesworth,

I have made another mistake, just as I did with the windows. I thought those were our roses or I wouldn't have picked them. I wanted to make it up to you.

Mom was right. She said I should have "let sleeping dogs lie." I thought she might be changing her mind about getting a dog, but she meant that trying to be friends with you would only lead to more trouble.

It's probably best if we don't exchange another word, like you and Mr. Thomas. That way nothing else can go wrong.

Your sad and silent neighbor,

P. S. McGinnity

P. S. McGinnity

Mom's magazine article was due. It had been difficult for her to find time to write while we were moving into our new house.

"Will you go to the post office for me, P. S.?" she asked. "You'll need to be quick. Oh, and here's some money. We need some milk as well."

I was on my way back when it happened. I had just passed Number 16 (somewhat cautiously), when a furry brown shape zoomed out the gate, closely followed by a woman waving a leash and shrieking, "Stop, Roly, stop!"

But the mysterious Roly was beyond stopping. He was on a collision course with my legs. Roly, the carton of milk, and I all went down in a heap. Luckily for me it was a soft landing! Dad had spent all weekend digging the front garden before planting his new seedlings, which were now being watered by the garden sprinkler.

I looked up from my bed of squashed seedlings. Staring back down at me was the shocked, saddened and recently soaked resident from next door, C. V. Molesworth.

"P. S. McGinnity?" She rapped out my name suddenly.

"Y-y-yes," I stammered.

"What does the P. S. stand for?"

I felt myself blushing through the milk. "Petunia Sylvania," I muttered. "It's stupid. Just call me P. S."

"It's a perfectly good name," she retorted.

Then I remembered Dad telling me that attack is the best form of defense. "So, what does C. V. stand for?" I demanded, with as much dignity as I could muster, with milk dripping from the end of my nose.

Now *she* looked embarrassed. She didn't want to answer, either. There was a long pause. "Charity Victoria," she mumbled. "Ridiculous name!"

"Charity is a perfectly good name, too," I said. I couldn't believe my eyes. C. V. Molesworth was actually blushing!

"Well, we'd better get you cleaned up, hadn't we," she said.

Much later, in dry clothes and after a long round of apologies from C. V. Molesworth, I found myself sitting on my neighbor's porch. By then she had replaced Mom's carton of milk and even offered to help Dad replant the front garden. (He graciously declined.)

C. V. Molesworth's porch was beautiful. There were hanging baskets of leafy plants and pots of bright geraniums. We sat on old cane chairs with faded velvet cushions. Wind chimes sounded softly in the breeze. And at my feet slept a worn-out brown puppy.

"I could guess from your letters that you wished you had a dog," C. V. Molesworth explained. "And that made me remember how much I used to enjoy having a dog around the place. I thought it would be good to have a watchdog, too, now that I'm on my own. So I went to the pound and picked out Roly. I was just about to take him for a walk when he saw you go past and dashed away from me," she said. "I'm very sorry about all the trouble we caused."

I told her I was sorry about the trouble I'd caused her, too. "I rush into things without thinking. It's a bad habit."

"Well, I suppose we both know now how it feels to be knocked down, covered with milk, and soaked through to the skin," said C. V. Molesworth.

"With a vandalized garden to add to the matter," I said, trying not to laugh. But it was too late; a chuckle escaped from the corner of my mouth. To my surprise, C. V. Molesworth was trying not to laugh, too. So we both stopped trying and really roared!

"You do like dogs, P. S., don't you?" said C. V. Molesworth, when we had finally calmed down enough to speak.

"Yes, but Mom won't let me have one. She says she likes her home to be peaceful."

C. V. Molesworth's eyes twinkled. "With you around? She must be joking!"

I didn't mind her saying that now that we were friends.

C. V. Molesworth leaned slightly toward me. "I tell you what, P. S.; I'd love it if you'd come over sometimes and help me with Roly. He certainly needs some training, and he definitely likes you."

The only trouble is, Roly has become such a good watchdog that he wants to scare *everyone* away from the place – even me!

"But where there's a will, there's a way," C. V. Molesworth says.

And I think she's right. We've worked out our "little" problems before – and I bet we can solve this one, too!

TITLES IN THE SERIES